Books with Stories and Pictures by DOROTHY P. LATHROP

Illustrated by DOROTHY P. LATHROP

BOUNCING BETSY

BY
DOROTHY P. LATHROP

THE MACMILLAN COMPANY
NEW YORK
1936

Printed in the United States of America by
Pace Press, Inc.

TO

HELEN R. LINSCOTT

BOUNCING BETSY

BETSY was bouncing over the fields. It was so early in the morning that her hoofs were wet with dew. Even her sides were wet where the grass had brushed against her wool, for she was a very little lamb.

"There will be lots and lots of other lambs for you to play with," said Martha comfortingly. "It will be like a party. *I'm* going to a party too. That's why I have to leave you all alone."

Of course Martha wasn't a sheep. She was a little girl, but she was used to being a mother to all sorts of creatures—puppies and kittens, and calves, and even little squealing pigs—but *they* all had real mothers besides. She was even mother to a big gray rabbit, who was too old to need one at all. But she was the only mother the little lamb had. So Betsy was being very careful not to lose sight of her in this big strange field.

"You won't be lonesome a bit—not with all those other lambs," said Martha. But she didn't feel very sure about it.

Betsy was so little. Martha could have counted all the few days of her life on one daisy's petals, only it was much too early for daisies. Just now there were violets and dandelions in the grass. There were apple blossoms overhead, and windflowers at the woods' edge.

In all her short life, Betsy had never been alone before. Not alone all day, that is. Not from sunrise to sunset.

"I'll be back before it's dark," promised Martha.

But Betsy wasn't listening. She was too busy kicking her heels in the air. Too busy making little sidewise jumps for no reason at all except that it was morning. Or bouncing very fast and high with her four legs all stiff and straight, her hoofs thumping softly on the close-cropped grass.

She couldn't help bouncing. That was why her name wasn't just plain Betsy, but Bouncing Betsy.

The cows looked up from their breakfast as, running and hopping, skipping and bouncing, Martha and Betsy crossed their pasture. The horses, too, lifted their heads, and whinnied and trotted after them as they ran, for Martha was a friend of theirs.

"*You'd* better not play with horses," said Martha, catching the little lamb up. "Their feet are too big."

Lazily the cows watched as they passed. All but Daisy, who heaved herself slowly and clumsily up from the ground and followed them with outstretched neck. She *had* to see what Martha was carrying and whether it was good to eat.

Curiously she sniffed the air behind them, and her breath blew in warm gusts through Martha's hair and down her neck. A long rough tongue reached out and raked the lamb's face from her woolly forehead to her chin. Betsy shut her eyes very tightly and her head thumped against Martha's chest.

"Go *away,* Daisy," scolded Martha, pushing at the cow's great, cold, wet, slippery nose.

"You'd better not play with cows either," she said. "Their horns are too long—and their tongues are too long too."

She lifted Betsy over the rails of the fence and climbed over after her. Daisy hung her head sadly over the bars and stared after them. Her jaws moved slowly from side to side.

"We're almost there," said Martha.

Betsy gave a little skip. She didn't care where she was as long as she was with Martha.

Already the two were halfway across the next pasture, a steep field that rolled right up against the sky, and then rolled down again. They raced each other to the top.

"Look, Betsy, look!" panted Martha.

Below them the little valley was white with sheep. Skipping and hopping around them, just as Betsy skipped and hopped around Martha, frisked dozens and dozens of little lambs. And up to the hilltop through that still morning air, floated a deep soft maaing, and a thin, high, many-toned baaing, and a little sharp clanging of bells.

"Now," said Martha, when at last they stood by the open gate, "now go and play with the other lambs." And she gave Betsy a little push.

Was this a new game? Betsy bounced right back again, and looked up trustfully into Martha's face. She didn't look at the lambs at all.

"You'll *like* playing with lambs," said Martha cheerfully. She didn't really feel very cheerful. She'd almost rather not go to the party than leave Betsy behind! She looked so much littler than the other lambs! Would they bump her too hard with their heads?

"Perhaps you'd better play with rabbits," she said anxiously, "or . . . or woodchucks—little ones—or squirrels."

Just inside the fence Martha carefully set Betsy's bottle all filled with milk.

"That's your dinner and your supper," she said.

She gave Betsy another little push, and suddenly the gate was shut between them.

"Baa!" protested Betsy, pushing against the bars.

"Have a good time at the party!" called Martha over her shoulder, running very fast.

"Baa! Baa! Baa! Baa-a-a-a-a-a!" shrieked Betsy, running back and forth along the fence. She couldn't push through it anywhere! And her mother was going home without her! Her mother was leaving her behind! She was disappearing over the top of the hill!

"BAA-A-A-A-A-A-A!"

Betsy was all alone.

And just then a great red sun rose over the trees that bordered the pasture, and Betsy's party day had begun.

Betsy didn't know anything about parties. She only knew that she was all alone, and that she didn't like it.

"Baa!" She didn't like it a bit.

The sheep stared at her. She was making more noise than all their lambs together.

"Baa!"

Even the lambs stared. They stopped frisking, and crowded around her and stared. And still Betsy cried for her mother.

The other lambs pushed her with their black bumpy foreheads. Their noses were black too, and so were their legs. They didn't look like Betsy, who was white all over. They bumped her hard and gamboled around her. But Betsy didn't want to play. She only wanted Martha.

They pushed her right away from the fence. They butted her until her ribs were sore and she had no breath for bleating. They played so roughly she gathered her legs together and bounced off over the pasture. She bounced because it was faster than running.

Soon she was all out of breath and her sore ribs heaved, for the pasture was very big. But she was safe. Now she could stop bouncing and look for her mother.

But Martha wasn't behind that tree with the white blossoms, nor in back of that rock. She wasn't even behind those big leaves.

But something was! Up popped a rabbit. Betsy jumped, and waited fearfully for it to butt her. But it only lifted its ears up straight and stared, and wiggled its nose and its whiskers. And so did all the little rabbits that crept out from under the leaves and from behind their mother.

How little they were! They made Betsy feel very big and brave. She touched one with her nose. It hopped! She poked it again. It ducked under a leaf. This was fun! She followed them around and poked one after another until they all hid under the leaves.

Then Betsy felt so brave that she put down her head and butted the big rabbit! The rabbit stamped angrily, shook her ears, and dived after her children.

Betsy tossed her head happily. She didn't feel nearly so small now as when the other lambs had pushed her about. Hadn't she butted rabbits right out of sight?

She even bounced a little as she trotted over the pasture looking behind every stone and bush and tree. But nowhere could she find Martha. So when she came to a fence, she squeezed until she got under.

Suddenly, Betsy's legs braced themselves to jump. For right there in front of her, a huge shape loomed. But where could she jump *to* with that creature before her and the fence right behind? So her legs wobbled.

Then Betsy saw that it was only a sheep, but one with great horns that curved out from a head that was proud with their weight.

What horns to butt with! But Betsy wasn't afraid. His face was white like hers, not black like the other lambs' faces. Timidly she edged up to him and, reaching as high as she could, buried her nose in his wool. But he looked right over her head as if she were a dandelion puff, or a weed not worth the eating.

So Betsy went on alone over a field all filled with rocks and hummocks.

The hummocks were soft and springy, and nicer for bouncing, but the rocks were so high that Betsy could see the whole world from their tops. Only sometimes she forgot to look for Martha because bouncing down again was such fun.

What a soft hummock! It heaved and squirmed under her sharp hoofs as she tried to keep her balance. Betsy stared down at it, and the hummock glared up at her and angrily rattled its long yellow teeth.

No wonder! It wasn't a hummock at all, but a woodchuck! Betsy fell off in surprise, and the woodchuck grumbled all the way to her hole and all the way down it. She even forgot her babies, or at least she left them behind her. So Betsy poked them and pushed them and nibbled their thick fur, and butted one until it rolled around like a ball.

She liked playing with woodchucks, but they didn't like playing with her. They squealed and waddled down the hole after their mother. And though Betsy peered down after them and waited, not one came up again out of the ground.

She didn't wait long. Off she went over the meadow, but found no more rabbits or woodchucks to play with. There were only rocks. And Betsy leaped over and scrambled up on them until the sun dried the dew on the grass.

But it wasn't much fun playing alone. Where was Martha? Betsy set off once more to find her. But no Martha answered her lonesome baa-ing.

The grass and the rocks were gone. Deep moss closed softly and damply around her hoofs. Ferns uncurled above the brown leaves.

"Baa!" called Betsy, all alone in the woods.

"Baa-a-a-a!" she blatted in alarm as a patch of brown leaves moved toward her.

But it wasn't leaves at all, but a fawn no bigger than Betsy. Its brown coat was dappled with spots as white as her wool. Betsy's ears drooped and her legs wobbled a little. Would the fawn butt her? No, it stood looking at Betsy, as little and timid as she was. They stretched out their necks until their noses touched.

The fawn's mother sniffed Betsy all over to be sure *she* wouldn't butt. Her gusty breath tickled Betsy's ears, and she shook them until they flapped and the tickle shook out.

All the while the fawn was darting around in little circles, begging Betsy to play. So Betsy dashed right out from under the deer's nose and followed. They leaped over fern fronds. They dashed around trees. This was more fun than butting!

Over clumps of gold cowslips where the ground was all squashy and wet, the fawn sailed, hardly wetting its hoofs. And Betsy bounced after, but all around *her,* the water splashed up in a shower!

How could a lamb hope to keep up long with a creature who flew like a bird, and who weighed hardly more than a small bunch of feathers? Betsy panted with wide-open mouth. Her legs flew in every direction.

Suddenly the fawn was gone. Had it heard its mother whistle? It was nowhere. Betsy called it with a little murmuring baa. Then she bleated.

There were only trees around her to answer. She couldn't even hear the other lambs baaing, or the faintest clanging of sheep bells.

Betsy was lost! She opened her mouth and blatted more loudly than she had ever blatted before. She ran back and forth among the trees crying until she was hoarse, until nothing but little husky, whispering baas came out of her throat.

Oh, if only there were something alive in these big woods!

Then she saw the fox standing motionless among the mandrake leaves, his very tail stiff with watching. But though his fur was redder than fallen hemlock needles, whiter than the mandrake flowers, and his legs blacker than any jutting root, she didn't like him at all!

She hated the way he looked at her with his sharp yellow eyes. His smell hurt her nostrils and her nose wrinkled up in disgust. It wasn't sweet like the smell of a lamb or a fawn, but all musty and horrid.

The fox licked his lips as if he was hungry. And suddenly, bleating with all the voice she had left, Betsy ran!

She ran faster than a fawn. And though she didn't know where she was running to, in no time at all her hoofs had left the silent moss and were thudding on the hard, close-cropped ground of the pasture. Over their swift drumming she could hear no baaing or tinkling of bells. But there, all at once, were the lambs and their mothers right below her.

She ran straight toward them. Oh, how she wanted to be safe among them! She was no longer afraid of their hard heads. What—afraid of *lambs* when in the woods there were foxes with red, hungry tongues?

As for the lambs' mothers, not one had horns that curled around and sprang out from her head in great spirals. *They* could know nothing about butting!

But Betsy knew lots! She had butted rabbits and woodchucks until they ran. Now she longed to butt lambs.

She didn't wait to crawl under the fence. She sailed over it. At full tilt she dashed down the hillside. With head down, she hurled herself straight at the fat ribs of a lamb lots bigger than she was, and knocked him right off his feet!

Betsy bounced in triumph. No lamb in the flock felt bigger. But she had to get her breath before she did any more butting. She was panting until her pink tongue showed and her ribs pushed up ridges in her short thick wool.

But oh, how glad she was to be back among sheep!

Then she danced on her hind legs to say she was ready to play. First on her hind, then on her front legs, while her tail flapped and flew every which way.

The lambs were delighted. They put down their black foreheads and rushed at her. But what lamb could touch her? She gamboled two times around them while they turned once on their clumsy black legs. She butted them hard, then skipped out of reach so that they lunged against air. One lamb, losing his balance, fell down on his knees and bumped his nose on the ground.

She was little, and thin, and quick as a grasshopper.

Even Martha couldn't be having a better time at her party than Betsy was having at hers!

Then Betsy ran off over the pasture with all the lambs after her. Their little quick feet beat like a sudden shower of hail on the hillside.

Their mothers lifted their pale eyes and stared without interest, never shifting their great bodies as the lambs hurtled past them.

The very biggest rock in the field, Betsy chose as her own and, scrambling up to its top, dared them to follow her. Not one, to be sure, had thought of climbing that rock until she claimed it. Now they all wanted to be on its top.

But as fast as they clambered up, Betsy battered them down again. And she wasn't at all careful *how* she did it!

She bumped their heads until the lambs slid down again backwards, their hoofs scraping noisily over the rough stone. She knocked little grunts right out of them. And she butted their rumps until they tucked their tails under them, doubled their legs, and leaped off into space.

But they loved it! *This* was the way to play! But not one dared stand on that rock until Betsy was tired of playing.

But even a lamb can't play forever. Betsy was hot, and she was thirsty. It was long past her dinner time. Never before had she gone without dinner. She looked around for it with a little hopeful baa that sounded like a question. But no Martha came carrying a bottle of warm milk.

Forlornly she tagged the flock down to the pond where geese and their goslings floated in spreading circles of ripples.

And when the sheep drank with sucking, gurgling noises that sounded to Betsy like the little noises she made over her own dinner, she was so thirsty that she too plunged her nose deep into the water.

But oh, it wasn't milk! And it was cold! And it got up her nose! She sputtered and shook her head in disgust again and again to get every last horrid drop off her nose.

All at once the pond at her feet was churned into leaping waves, and the whole sky was filled with great beating wings. Long necks curved and darted toward her. Clashing beaks snapped in her face and her ears were filled with a loud hissing.

Betsy ran! Oh, how she ran!

She ran until she was safe in the midst of the flock. She darted between forests of legs and wedged herself between high walls of warm, comforting woolly sides where she could see no wings beating. And there she stayed until her legs stopped trembling.

How could she know that the geese were afraid she would hurt their goslings? She had only wanted her dinner.

All around her the other lambs were down on their knees having supper. Betsy grew hungrier and hungrier. *They* had had dinner and supper and lots of snacks in between, but she had had nothing.

She had quite forgotten, if she had ever noticed, the bottle Martha had left by the fence.

Betsy bleated imploringly, but not a single lamb would move over to make room for her. And each sheep knew its own lamb, and none would give Betsy a drop of milk. Though she begged with outstretched neck and hopefully fluttering tail, they all pushed her away with their heads.

If only she could find her own mother! Betsy wandered back to the fence. There was the place she had tried to push through. There were the same dandelion puffs—but no Martha. Only a mother raccoon and her three babies.

But wasn't that Betsy's own bottle the big raccoon was holding up in her paws? Betsy's dinner she was lapping? The lamb ran toward it with a joyful blat. Oh, how hungry she was!

But the raccoon did not offer it to Betsy—did not hold it for her as Martha did. Instead, she whined and curled back her lips until her teeth showed. And Betsy backed away, ears drooping. She looked on sadly as the milk gurgled out of the tipped-up bottle and spilled into a white pool on the ground, where the little raccoons lapped it up as fast as they could.

Betsy looked at it. Timidly, she stuck her nose into it. But it too was cold, and it too got up her nose as the pond did. Sputtering, she shook it off. She only knew how to drink out of bottles.

And Betsy's dinner soaked into the ground.

The sun was going down over the hillside, big and red as it had come up. And once more the dew was cool on the grass.

Under the trees, white with their blossoms, the sheep were folding their short legs under them and settling themselves for the night.

They stared over the meadow, watching with quiet eyes. Slowly, slowly their jaws moved back and forth without stopping. Now and then a bell jangled softly.

Close against their great sides, warmed by deep wool, sprawled their lambs, eyes drooping, heads heavy. Not a bounce was left in their limp heels. Twilight had stilled all their bleatings.

And from the pond, high and silvery sweet, rang the shrill din of the peepers.

It was almost dark, but still Betsy stood by the fence and peered through it, waiting and watching for Martha.

And she shivered a little in her short wool. Lower and lower drooped her sleepy head. But again and again she jerked it up to stare between the rails. So she stood gazing until her legs swayed beneath her and her eyes closed all of themselves.

She alone had no thick-fleeced mother to warm her, so she curled up as close as she could to the fence.

The moon came up over the field behind it. It rose higher than the topmost rail, and still Betsy slept.

An owl floated on silent wings down to the fence, an owl as big as the small lamb on the ground beneath him. But even his stare did not wake her.

Neither did his claws nor his hungry beak. Silently he spread his wings wide and was gone as he heard Martha coming over the pasture.

"Betsy! Betsy! Betsy!" she called as she came.

Betsy, joggling over the fields in Martha's arms, opened her eyes a crack. Then she opened them wide.

"Mmmmm-m-m-m," Betsy murmured drowsily without opening her mouth. "Mmmmm-m-m-m, mmmmm-m-m-m, mmmmm-m-m-m," as if she could never stop.

She had a mother again!

"*Poor* Betsy, are you hungry?" asked Martha.

"Mmmmm-m-m-m, mmmmm-m-m-m," said Betsy again, hopefully nibbling Martha's chin and bumping it with her nose.

"And did you have a good time at your party? *I* had ice cream and cake."

"Mmmmm-m-m-m-m-m," replied Betsy.

"*We* played games. Did you play with the other lambs any? And did they bump you too hard with their heads?"

But Betsy's eyes were closing again.

"And did you bounce just as much as you wanted to?" asked Martha.

"Mmm-m-m-m," murmured Betsy very softly.

And all the way home her head bumped sleepily against Martha's chest.

D.P.L.

The End

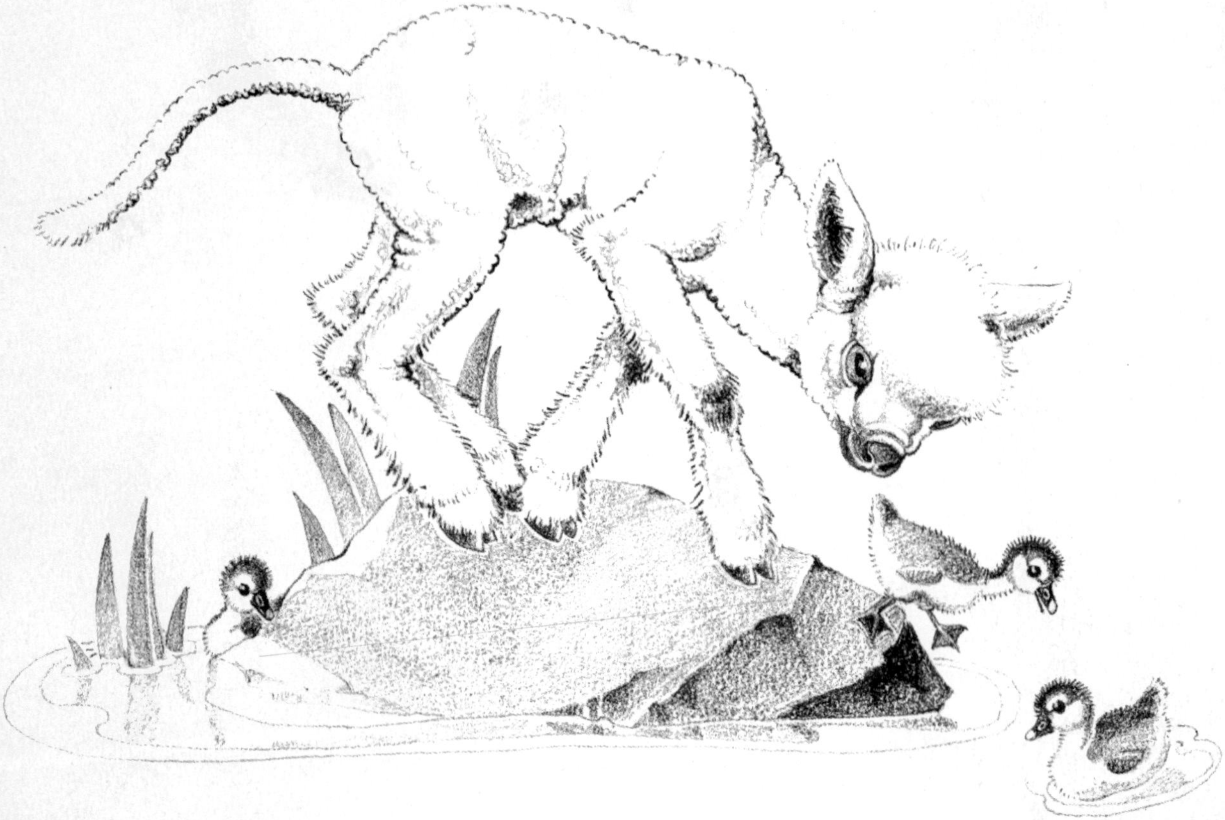